Cale Atkinson

Off & Away

Disney • HYPERION

Los Angeles   New York

Out at sea, there is a place
where all the messages in bottles gather.

Jo's dad made sure every bottle
got to the right home.

He always returned with a new story
of adventure to share.

Jo wanted to be a great
adventurer just like him.

There was only one thing that kept her
from getting out on the seas . . .

... a fear of what lurked below.

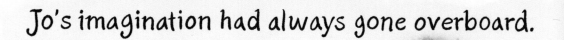

Jo's imagination had always gone overboard.

So as much as she wanted to,
she never joined her dad out at sea.

And that's the way things were, until . . .

Day after day he tried heading out,

but he needed rest.

Bottles began
to pile up.

Everyone was counting on him.
If he couldn't deliver,
then who could?

Jo's legs were shaking like jellyfish, and sea butterflies filled her insides from head to toe.

One at a time, she carefully loaded the bottles into the boat.

Taking a deep breath in . . .

I can do this. I
I can do this. I can d
do this. I can do this. I
do this. I can do
I can do this.
this. I ca
I can do this. I can do th
I an do this. I c
I can do this. I can do
I can do this. I can do this.
I can do this. I can
I can do this. I can do t
I can do this. I
I can do this.
I can do this

I can do this. I can do this.
I can do this. I can
do this. I can do
this.
is. I can do this. I can do th
can do this. I can
o this. I can do this.
I can do this. I can do this.
do this. I can do this.
is. I can do this. I can
I can do this. I can do this.
this. I can do this. I can do th
I can do this. I can do this.
do this. I can do this.
I can do this.
do this. I can
I can do this
this

she cast off.

As she sailed toward her first delivery, tentacles full of sticky suckers curled out of the water.

Jo was certain
this would be the end of her!

But wait.
It was a squid named Ira.

The next delivery was for a beast
big as an island!

Oh! It WAS an island.

Before long, the monsters Jo kept seeing . . .

disappeared.

Only one bottle was left.
But this one was different.
This bottle was for Blackwater Bay.

A place even Jo's dad
hadn't sailed.

Treacherous waters and sunken ships
surrounded the dark bay.

The winds grew stronger, and the sea tossed Jo like a minnow.

The boat was driftwood. The last bottle was gone.
And worst of all, she had let her dad down.

Things couldn't get worse. . . .

Or could they?

This time it wasn't her imagination.

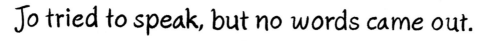

Jo tried to speak, but no words came out.

The gigantic creature turned to leave.
"WAIT!" she shouted. "This is for you!"

"Holy tuna! Could it be?"
The monster carefully pulled a lightbulb out from the bottle.
"Gosh, it's been so lonely here in the dark.
No one has dared sail here to deliver a new bulb."

In an instant, the bay lit up.

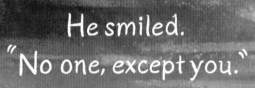

He smiled.
"No one, except you."

Soon the bay filled with visitors,
guided by the lighthouse.
To show his thanks,
Jo's new friend did his best to repair her boat.
"It's the least I can do!" he said.

Jo set sail for home . . .

...and returned with a monster of a story to share.

Dedicated to those who don't let their fears stop them
from the great adventures that await.

First Edition, June 2018 | 10 9 8 7 6 5 4 3 2 1
FAC-019817-18110 | Printed in Malaysia

This book was hand-lettered by the author, and additional text
was set in Avenir LT Pro Light/Monotype.
The artwork was rendered with salt water, squid ink,
and Photoshop.

Reinforced binding
Visit www.DisneyBooks.com

Library of Congress Cataloging-in-Publication Data

Names: Atkinson, Cale, author, illustrator. | Title: Off & away / Cale
Atkinson. | Other titles: Off and away | Description: First edition.
• Los Angeles ; New York : Disney-Hyperion, 2018. | Summary: Jo
fears what lives in the ocean but when her father is too ill to deliver
messages in bottles, she courageously takes on the job, making
new friends along the way. | Identifiers: LCCN 2017014587 •
ISBN 9781484782323 (hardcover) • ISBN 1484782321 (hardcover)
Subjects: CYAC: Ocean bottles—Fiction. • Postal service—Fiction.
• Marine animals—Fiction. • Fear—Fiction. | Classification: LCC
PZ7.A86372 Off 2018 • DDC [E]—dc23 | LC record available at
https://lccn.loc.gov/2017014587